Books by Marcus Pfister

THE CHRISTMAS STAR*
DAZZLE THE DINOSAUR*
HOPPER*
HANG ON, HOPPER!
HOPPER HUNTS FOR SPRING*
HOPPER'S EASTER SURPRISE
HOPPER'S TREETOP ADVENTURE
HOW LEO LEARNED TO BE KING
I SEE THE MOON
MILO AND THE MAGICAL STONES*
PENGUIN PETE*
PENGUIN PETE AND LITTLE TIM*
PENGUIN PETE AND PAT*
PENGUIN PETE'S NEW FRIENDS*
PENGUIN PETE, AHOY!*
THE RAINBOW FISH*
RAINBOW FISH TO THE RESCUE!*
SHAGGY
SUN AND MOON*
WAKE UP, SANTA CLAUS!

*also available in Spanish

First published in Great Britain, Australia and New Zealand in 1988 by North-South Books,
an imprint of Nord-Süd Verlag AG, Gossau Zürich, Switzerland.
First paperback edition published in 1995.
Distributed in the United States by North-South Books Inc., New York

Library of Congress Cataloging-in-Publication Data
Pfister, Marcus.
Penguin Pete's New Friends / Marcus Pfister.
[1. Penguins—Fiction.] I. Title
87-72037

British Library Cataloging-In-Publications Data
Pfister, Marcus
Penguin Pete's New Friends
1. Title I. Pits neue Freunde. English
833'.914[J]   PZZ7

ISBN 1-55858-025-5 (trade binding)
5 7 9 11 TB 10 8 6
ISBN 1-55858-244-4 (library binding)
5 7 9 11 LB 10 8 6 4
ISBN 1-55858-414-5 (paperback)
5 7 9 PB 10 8 6 4
Printed in Belgium

For more information about our books, and the authors and artists
who create them, visit our web site: http://www.northsouth.com

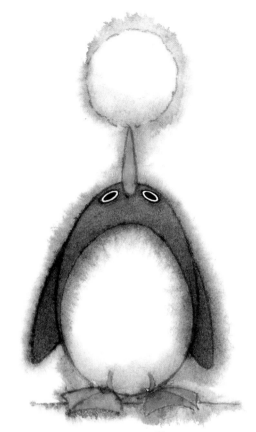

Marcus Pfister

Penguin Pete's
New Friends

Translated by Anthea Bell

North-South Books
New York / London

Penguin Pete was angry.

"If you won't let me go fishing with the big penguins, I'll go fishing by myself," he told his mother. "I expect to be gone a long time and to catch a lot of fish."

Pete's mother smiled. "Just be home in time for dinner," she said. She and some of the little penguins said goodbye as Pete left.

"I'll show them I'm grown up," said Pete. He made a running start and did a somersault into the water. The dive was a great success but he felt very tired. Luckily he saw a small island where he could rest.

As he sat on the island the sun shone on Pete's face. It felt so good, he decided to take a nap. As he drifted off to sleep, he began to have a wonderful dream about gliding through the water.

When Pete woke up, something was not right at all. A powerful jet of water had sent him flying into the air.

"Hello up there, little fellow," boomed a great voice below. "My name is Walter Whale. What are you doing on my back?"

"I was going fishing," said Pete, "but now I'm finished. I think I'll go home."

"That will be a long swim for a little fellow like you," said the whale. "Why don't you go fishing with me?"

Pete was thrilled. Wait until his mother heard that he had gone fishing with the largest creature in the ocean!

Walter swam north with Pete on his back. At last the two of them reached an island. Walter suggested that Pete have a look around.

Pete saw a boy dangling his fishing line into a hole in the ice. He had to laugh.

"Hello, little boy," he said. "I'm Pete. I'll show you a much easier way to catch fish."

Down Pete went into the hole in the ice, head first. Then, suddenly, he was stuck. Heaving and hauling, the boy managed to get him out.

"You're a funny fellow," said the boy. "I think we've done enough fishing for today. Let's go for a sleigh ride."
   The sleigh ride was fantastic.

The boy introduced Pete to an elephant seal. They got on famously.

But Pete's favorite animals were the sea lions.

One of the sea lions made a snowball and balanced it on his nose.
  "I can do that too," said Pete. Pete tried it, but before he
knew it his face was covered with snow.
  "Never mind!" said the sea lion laughing. "Everything's hard
when you first try it."

By nightfall Pete was safely on Walter's back returning home. It had been a wonderful fishing trip, even if he didn't catch any fish.